Get the companion song!

Purchase or hear a clip of the song “The First to See: Mary’s Easter Story” at https://alainalarsen.com/books/the-first-to-see/

Use this QR code to take you directly to the MP3 link.

To
mothers who encourage us
daughters who enliven us
friends who applaud us
husbands who reassure us
kids who pace us
Mary who inspires us
and our Savior who loves us

ISBN 13: 978-1-4621-4313-9

Published by CFI, an imprint of Cedar Fort, Inc.
2373 W. 700 S., Suite 100, Springville, UT 84663
Distributed by Cedar Fort, Inc., www.cedarfort.com

Cover design and interior layout by Shawnda T. Craig

Printed in the United States of America

10 9 8 7 6 5 4 3 2 1

Printed on acid-free paper

The First to See

·Mary's Easter Story·

written by Alaina Larsen and Cris Conerty
Illustrated by Althea Botha

CFI · An imprint of Cedar Fort, Inc. · Springville, Utah

As Jesus walked the earth and taught,
some women followed Him.

A faithful one among them was called
Mary Magdalene.

And she was near when He was crucified upon the cross.
As His disciple, loved by Him, she deeply mourned His loss.

The garden tomb was sealed up
and the watchmen tarried there,

while Mary, with devotion,
special spices did prepare.

Then, at the third day's dawning,

Mary went to where Christ lay.

To her surprise, she found the stone
already rolled away!

Inside the tomb, His linen cloth
had carefully been laid.
And there, in shining garments,
stood an angel who did say,

"Why do you seek to find
the living here among the dead?

"He is not here!

"Go tell that He has risen, as He said!"

So, Mary told her Lord's Apostles,
who ran to the place.

And after seeing for themselves,
they went away amazed!

Now, Mary would become the first
to see the Risen Christ

when, in the garden, He appeared
before her very eyes!

But she, supposing Him the gardener, asked Him tearfully
if He knew where the body of her precious Lord could be.

Then, when the Resurrected Savior,
in love, spoke her name,

she cried out, “Master!” knowing
He had come to life again!

The First to See: Mary's Easter Story

Words and Music by Alaina Larsen and Cris Conerty

Vocal Solo with Piano and/or Guitar

Mat. 27: 56, 61
Mat. 28:1
John 20: 14-18

Am G Am
lene. And she was near when He was cru - ci -
pare. Then, at the third day's dawn - ing, Ma - ry
say, "Why do you seek to find the liv - ing
mazed! Now, Ma - ry would be - come the first to
be. Then, when the res - ur - rect - ed Sav - ior,
G/B G7 Dm/F Esus7 E7/B Am G/B
fied u - pon the cross. As His dis - ci - ple,
went to where Christ lay. To her sur - prise, she
here a - mong the dead? He is not here! Go
see the Ris - en Christ, when, in the gar - den,
in love, spoke her name, she cried out, "Mas - ter!"
C
loved by Him, she
found the stone al -
tell that He has
He ap - peared be -
know - ing He had
1, 2, 3, 4.
F6 Gsus G Am
deep - ly mourned His loss.
read - y rolled a - way!
ri - sen, as He said!"
fore her ve - ry eyes!
5.
Dm/F E7 Am G/B C Dm E7 A
come to life a - gain!

Mary Magdalene

Mary Magdalene was from Magdala, a city on the western shore of the Sea of Galilee. After Jesus miraculously healed her, she became a devoted disciple and respected leader among the early Christians.

(Matt. 27:56, 61; 28:1; Mark 15:40, 47; 16:1, 9; Luke 8:2; 24:10; John 19:25; 20:1, 14–18)

Who were Mary's Friends?

Joanna

Like Mary, Joanna was healed by Jesus. As the wife of Chuza, the household steward of the Roman ruler Herod Antipas, Joanna used her influence and wealth to support the ministry of Jesus.

(Luke 8:2–3; 24:10)

The "Other Mary"

Mary was called the "Other Mary" to distinguish her from Mary Magdalene and Mary, the mother of Jesus. Mary was a popular name! This Mary was the wife of Cleophas and the mother of the Apostle James "the Younger" and his brother Joses.

(Matt. 15:40, 47; 16:1; 27:56, 61; 28:1; Luke 24:10; John 19:25)

Salome

Salome was the wife of Zebedee, a prosperous fisherman, and the mother of Apostles James and John the Beloved. She was one of the first to believe in the divine mission of the Messiah.

(Matt. 20:20–23; 27:56, 61; 28:1, Mark 15:40; 16:1)

Other Women

The scriptures also speak of Mary, the mother of Jesus, who was at the cross, present at many miraculous occasions and a constant influence and participant in the Savior's life. In addition, Susanna, who became a devoted convert to Christ after a miraculous healing, is mentioned (Luke 8:1–3), as well as many other unnamed women (Mark 15:41; Luke 8:3; 24:10). Although these women are not specifically named as being present at the immediate events leading up to the resurrection, we know they, too, rejoiced in the miracle of Easter.